EGMONT

We bring stories to life

First published in Great Britain in 2008 by Dean,
an imprint of Egmont UK Limited
239 Kensington High Street, London W8 6SA

Thomas the Tank Engine & Friends™

CREATED BY BRITT ALLCROFT

Based on the Railway Series by the Reverend W Awdry
© 2008 Gullane (Thomas) LLC. A HIT Entertainment company.
Thomas the Tank Engine & Friends and Thomas & Friends are trademarks of Gullane (Thomas) Limited.
Thomas the Tank Engine & Friends and Design is Reg. U.S. Pat. & Tm. Off.

HiT entertainment

ISBN 978 0 6035 6320 1
1 3 5 7 9 10 6 4 2
Printed in Singapore

Salty's Secret

The Thomas TV Series

DEAN

All the engines on the Island of Sodor love their work. But sometimes there is so much work to do that they need some help.

One day, The Fat Controller decided to bring Salty the Dockside Diesel to help out at the Quarry.

Salty was excited about coming to the Island of Sodor because it was surrounded by the sea.

Salty loved the sea and had worked at lots of different Docks the world over. He had many seaside tales to tell and loved to share them with his Driver.

Soon, Salty arrived at his new job. Mavis was there with the twin engines, Bill and Ben.

"Ahoy there, mateys! I'm Salty, pride of the seven seas!" he called cheerfully. "I'm the new diesel and I'm here to give you some help."

Bill and Ben didn't think they needed any help. Especially from a diesel!

"Welcome to the Quarry," said Mavis.
Salty looked all around. Everywhere he looked, he
saw rocks.

"A quarry?" he cried. "There must be some mistake.
I'm a Dockside diesel."

"You're a quarry diesel now,"
said Mavis.

Mavis explained that they only had three days to complete an important job for The Fat Controller.

Salty was sad he wouldn't be working by the sea. But he wanted to show that he was a Really Useful Engine.

"Ah, well," said Salty, "at least there are trucks."

"You'd better be careful with them," Mavis said.
"They can be very naughty."

Bill and Ben were listening to Mavis.
"He won't last five minutes," huffed Bill.
"Those trucks will trip him up soon enough,"
agreed Ben.

But the trucks gave Salty no trouble at all. Bill and Ben couldn't understand it!

"Yo, ho, ho and a bucket of prawns," Salty sang, as he pushed the trucks. "The tiller spins . . ."

". . . and the Captain yawns!" sang the trucks. Salty could pull twice as many trucks as Bill and Ben.

By the end of the day, The Fat Controller's important job was almost done.

Bill and Ben were very surprised . . . and a little bit jealous. That night, they saw Salty stop outside the shed.

"Here comes Mr Show-off," grumbled Ben.

"Don't be silly! Salty is wonderful with those trucks," said Mavis.

"Driver says he'll bore the bolts off us with his stories," said Bill.

Outside, Salty was humming an old sea song.

Mavis rolled alongside Salty. "What are you doing out here on your own?" she asked.

"Oh, I thought I might catch a bit of the sea breeze," said Salty, sadly.

"You really do miss the sea, don't you?" said Mavis.

"Aye," said Salty. "I do." But he knew that the Quarry work was important.

The next day, Salty tried to show Bill and Ben his secret with the trucks.

"I like working to music," he said. "And so do the trucks. Why don't you sing songs with them, like me?"

Bill and Ben tried, but they still could not move the trucks the way Salty could.

Later that day, The Fat Controller came to the Quarry. He was surprised to see that the job had been finished.

"Well done, everyone," he said.

"It was Salty," said Mavis. "We couldn't have done it without him."

"Then I've got another job for you, Salty," said The Fat Controller.

"Aye aye, Sir," sighed Salty. "Which quarry am I going to this time?"

"Quarry?" said The Fat Controller. "It's not a quarry at all. I'm sending you to Brendam Docks!"

"The Docks?" cried Salty, happily. "The Docks are just by the sea! Oh, thank you, Sir!"

Salty loved Brendam Docks. He got more work done than three other engines put together.

"I'm a Really Useful Engine," he said to himself, proudly.

And all the other engines had to agree!